Jack Goes to Montessori School

Allyson Collins
Illustrations by Lindsey R. Smith

Jack Goes to Montessori School

By
Allyson Collins

Buena Austin Publishing

ISBN: 978-0-9898235-0-0

For J, my love and inspiration – A.C.

To Audrey and Beverly who introduced me
to the world of art and teaching – L.R.S.

Hi! I'm Jack.

I am four years old and I go to Montessori school.

When I get to school, I say goodbye to my Mom and go to my classroom.

I love to see my teachers and friends!

I am in a Primary class, and my classmates are different ages. Some of my friends have just joined us from the Toddler class, some are my age, and some friends are in kindergarten.

At the start of each day, my class has circle time.
I sit criss-cross applesauce while my teachers read a story,
sing songs, give lessons, or lead us in show-and-tell.

Today in circle time, we are having a group lesson.
Our class has been learning about the planets all week,
and today, we talk about the planet Saturn!

After circle time, it is Montessori work time. There is so much fun work in my class, and I get to choose what I want to do! My friends also choose their own work. Sometimes I work with my friends, but I also like to work by myself.

Our teachers always give us a lesson on how to do each work, and I ask questions if I need help.

When I work on the floor, I first get a work mat from the basket and carry it to my workspace. I unroll the mat on the floor and then choose my work.

I like letters, so I start with language work today.
First, I work on sandpaper letters. I trace each letter with
my finger to learn the shape and then I say
the sound of the letter. I know all of the sounds!

The moveable alphabet is challenging work and helps me learn how to spell using letter sounds. Look – I spelled my name!

Don't forget to put away your work and mat when you are done!

I move on to my favorite work, the geography puzzle maps.
I have been working on the continent maps,
and I already finished Africa and Asia!

Today, I work on the North America puzzle map.

I see where I live!

Next, I build the pink tower with one of my friends.
We stack the cubes from largest to smallest and then count
the cubes from one to ten forwards and backwards.

The puzzle maps and the pink tower are types of sensorial work,
which help develop my senses, concentration, and attention.

I'm hungry, so I'm glad it is time for lunch!
Before we eat, I help set the table for my class.

After I am finished eating, I clean up my dishes.

Yay, it is playground time!
I love to slide and play chase with my friends.

I make a circle with my arms and spin around,
pretending to be Saturn with its rings.

Around and around ... I'm dizzy!

I am tired from being Saturn, so it is nice to take a rest.
I brought my favorite blanket and stuffed tiger
from home to help me sleep.

Zzzzz

After nap, my class does group activities like art, yoga, or music.
Today, we learn to solve problems with the Peace Flower.
My teacher asks me to help her with an example.

I pretend that I am upset with a classmate, and I get the
Peace Flower. I tell my friend what happened and how I feel.

Then, my friend takes the Peace Flower
and tells me how she feels.
We listen to each other and talk about our problem.

Once our problem is solved, my friend and I both hold
the Peace Flower and say, "we declare peace!"

Next, I get a snack while my teacher tells me about my classroom chore for this week.

I sweep with my friend. Our teacher is so happy because we work together respectfully and peacefully.

I'm ready for math!

My teacher gives me a lesson on the number rods.

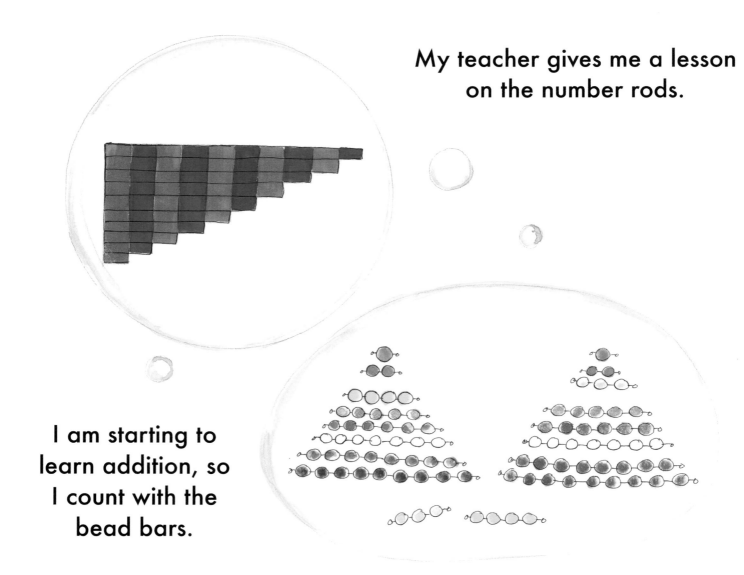

I am starting to learn addition, so I count with the bead bars.

Practical life work helps me learn to take care of myself and my environment.

I like to do pouring work, and today I choose to water a plant in my classroom. I clean up some water that spills.

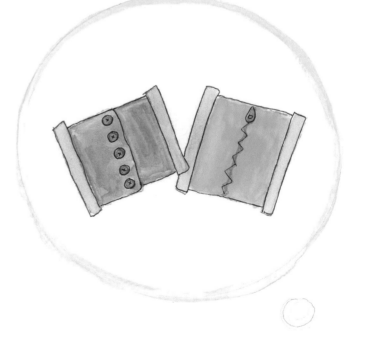

I also work on buttoning and using a zipper, because I want to learn how to put on my coat all by myself.

My Dad is here, so it is time to go home.

There is so much fun and challenging work at school, and I can't wait to try more tomorrow.

I really love Montessori school!

a b c 1 2 3

t h e e n d

Allyson Collins is an attorney and Montessori Mom who lives with her family (including one precocious redhead) in Austin, Texas. After first being introduced to the Montessori educational philosophy, Allyson was inspired to bring Jack's story to life in order to help other parents and children learn what makes the Montessori experience special.

Lindsey R. Smith (aka LRSmith ART) is a native Texan who has always had a passion for art and teaching. She began drawing comics as a child and is now a selling artist in the heart of Texas. Not only is Lindsey passionate about art, but she is a certified Montessori Teacher, as well as an Art Teacher for young children, and holds the Montessori philosophy dear to her heart. The children are her inspiration, so she is happy to share with you her illustrations of the joy and happiness found within a Montessori child.

Made in United States
Troutdale, OR
09/04/2023

12623168R00021